Books by the same author

The Magic Boathouse

For older readers

Pig in the Middle

The Rope School

SAM LLEWELLYN

Illustrations by Arthur Robins

WALKER BOOKS
AND SUBSIDIARIES
LONDON • BOSTON • SYDNEY

For Jonathon Green

First published 1998 by
Walker Books Ltd, 87 Vauxhall Walk
London SE11 5HJ

2 4 6 8 10 9 7 5 3 1

Text © 1998 Sam Llewellyn
Illustrations © 1998 Arthur Robins

The right of Sam Llewellyn to be identified as author of this
work has been asserted by him in accordance with the Copyright,
Designs and Patents Act 1988.

This book has been typeset in Garamond.

Printed in England

British Library Cataloguing in Publication Data
A catalogue record for this book
is available from the British Library.

ISBN 0-7445-4157-3

CONTENTS

RUMBLE OF HUNGER

Jack and Anna were on a cross-country hike. They had been trudging along since early morning. They were both a bit tired and a bit cross.

In Anna's mind was a single thought: "Must be lunchtime," she said.

"It's all right," said Jack. "I've brought a picnic."

That was what Anna had been afraid of. Jack was her own dear brother, but he had a weakness. He was a terrible cook, though he thought he was brilliant, and planned to be a Chef when he grew up.

Anna changed the subject. "Look! A fox!" she said.

Jack nodded. It was a badger. Anna was his own dear sister, but she had a weakness. She was

terrible at animals, though she
thought she was brilliant,
and planned to be a Wildlife Expert
when she grew up.

The day had turned gloomy and big drops of rain were falling. Jack and Anna headed into a wood. Under the trees it was dark, and the leaves dripped sullenly.

"Look!" cried Anna. "A mushroom!"

"If it's a mushroom," said Jack, "how come there's smoke coming out of it?"

"Mushrooms produce spores, not smoke," said Anna. "Look! A badger hole, or sett, as we call it!"

"If it's a badger sett, how come it's got a green door with a brass knocker?" said Jack, trying not to sound sarcastic. He sat down on a rotten log and opened his backpack. "Lunch," he said. "Sandwiches à la cheese. Sausages à la fried, served cold."

"Oh, great," said Anna, trying not to sound sarcastic. The sandwiches would be stale; they always were, when Jack made them. And the sausages would be half raw; they always were, when Jack fried them.

Grey vapour puffed from the mushroom.

"*Definitely* smoke," said Jack. "And a door." He pocketed his sandwich and went to investigate.

The mushroom was not a
mushroom. It was a small iron
chimney with a small
iron hat on it to keep
the rain out. The
smoke smelled
of frying onions,
toast, hot chocolate,
china tea and other
delicious stuff.

Jack found he was suddenly extra hungry. The lunch he had made was great, of course. But...

Anna went to look at the door in the hole. It was definitely green, with a definite knocker and a definite spyhole and a definite brass plate on it that said *Café*. Not wildlife, she thought. Not nature. But possibly lunch.

Lunch?

Café

It had started to rain again.

"Go on," said Jack, crossly.

"*All right*," said Anna, cross herself.
She grasped the knocker and beat
a sharp rat-a-tat.

SANDWICHES A LA FRIED

"'snot locked!" screeched a voice.
"Shove and enter!"

Jack shoved. They went in.

It was a hole. The walls were made of earth. There was a huge wood-burning cooker and a kitchen table. By the stove stood an animal with round ears, button eyes and a long white apron.

It's raining.

"Sorry," said Anna. "It's raining out there. Can we eat our lunch in the dry?"

"'course," said the animal. "What you got?"

"Sandwiches," said Anna, "à la cheese."

"*Yuk*," said the animal. "Bet they're stale."

"And sausages," said Jack, nettled, "à la fried."

"*Gak!* Call that lunch?" said the
animal. "Come over here."

"Why?" said Jack. It was upsetting
to have remarks made about your
cooking. Also the animal was
slightly bigger than him and had
very sharp-looking teeth.

Anna had not noticed the teeth.
"'scuse me," she said. "You're an
otter, aren't you?"

"Polecat, fool!" said the animal.
"The polecat is the animal that loves
to cook. Next thing you'll tell me
you thought my stove chimney was

22

a mushroom or somethin'."

"She did, actually," said Jack, feeling better. It was hard to be suspicious of a polecat who seemed to be turning out kindly as well as gruff.

"Now then. Give us your lunches."

"Hey!" said Jack.

"Sure," said Anna.

The polecat unwrapped, sniffed and made faces. "Bread, grease, slime. You can't eat that muck. Unless... " he said, hauling a gold watch from his apron pocket and glancing at it – "five to one. Well, why not?"

He grabbed a frying pan from a
hook on the wall, banged it on
to the stove, sloshed in a dose
of green oil, chopped a couple of
onions, softened
them, added
salt, pepper
and the sausages,
cut into cubes.

When the sausages were done he tossed in the cheese sandwiches, quartered, and fried them until the bread turned gold and the cheese started to ooze out at the sides. All the time, he talked. "Olive oil, pinch it from the vicar's larder. Onions from Mrs Jenkins' garden. Salt, pepper. Whoops, it's time."

He slammed the frying pan under the grill. Then he pointed to a rope that dangled through a hole in the ceiling. "Heave ho!" he said. "Then lunch."

Mouths watering, for the smell from under the grill was most delicious, Jack and Anna latched on to the rope and heave hoed.

Up above, a bell, hung from the
branch of a hollow tree, began to
toll. The forest floor came suddenly
alive. Across the musty leaves
trotted a stream of animals:

hedgehogs, rabbits, an orang-utan,
several foxes, stoats and weasels,
two armadillos and a single Chinese
pheasant with an inscrutable
expression on its face.

Each and every one of them was carrying a knife and fork except for the Chinese pheasant, which was carrying chopsticks.

In the trunk of the hollow tree where the bell hung was a sign that Jack and Emma had not seen.

It said: Café Customers' Entrance.

The animals filed in.

Silence fell.

But from the deep trees by the chapel came a low, vast sound. The sound of a mighty stomach. Rumbling.

THE POLECAT CAFE

Jack and Anna polished off their
plates of fried sausage, cheese
sandwich and onion in record time.

"Smashing," said Anna.

"Brilliant," said Jack.

"Can't beat a good lunch, I always say," said the polecat gruffly. "Well, mustn't sit here gossiping all day. Lend a hand my young shavers." He started hauling pots and pans out of various ovens and slamming them down on the table. Then he banged open a sliding hatch over the kitchen wall.

Beyond the hatch was a big room
with half a dozen long tables. At the
tables were sitting an enormous
number of animals.

As Jack watched, a handful of
earth fell down a wall and a mole
hopped out of a tunnel and on

to one of the benches.

"Use the Customers' Entrance like anyone else!" yelled the polecat.

There were grinnings and sniggerings. *Chefs*, the animals seemed to be saying. *Always cross about something.*

"Dish it out, then," said the polecat. So Anna and Jack began to dish it out.

"Loverly grubs," said a hedgehog.

"Lovely *grub*, porcupine," said Anna, correcting him.

"'edge'og to you," said the hedgehog. "I 'opes there's more than one grub in there."

"'course there is," said the polecat crossly. "Fuss, fuss."

Anna smiled weakly, trying not to look at the stew.

Jack was already giving seconds
to an orang-utan in a black suit and
dark glasses, who was gobbling
fried banana and
making notes in
a small book.
When the ape
had finished
his seconds,
he wiped his
rubbery lips
with his
napkin and
shambled off.

"Him!" the polecat sighed. "Every time the circus comes by, he's here, that one. Tells his posh friends about us. Me, I can't understand a word 'e says.

Once you get a name, you get sloths, armadillos, you name it. Shocking riff-raff, really, upsetting me regulars." He wagged his head. "But it's a slippery slope. Turn one away, well, yer café's empty ever after."

The last of the animals had left.
Jack and Anna were feeling better.

"Thank you very much," said Jack
politely, shouldering his pack.
"We'd better be off – " at that
moment, the ground shook.

BOOM, went something
overhead. BOOM, BOOM, BOOM.
Earth trickled from the ceiling.

VERY WILD LIFE

"What's *that*?" said Anna.

"Footsteps," said the polecat. "Rex.
Come for 'is lunch. Nothing left, of
course. It's always the same. He's so
slow, I can't be bothered with him.
Plus, he upsets the other customers.
Well, he's too late today."

"That's all right," said Jack, dropping his pack. "I'll make him some lunch."

The polecat looked suddenly rather cunning. "Why not?" he said. "Just a sandwich, mind. *Big* sandwich. Bread's over there."

"Hey – " said Anna, for Jack really was a terrible cook.

Why not?

Too late. Jack had donned an
apron, crammed on a spare hat and
ransacked the cupboards. "A really
good cook can make the best of
very few ingredients," he said,
scraping the mould off a stale loaf
and sawing it open.

Humming a little tune, he slathered the bread with margarine, cut up six rotten tomatoes, some raw onions and a tin of dog food. Then he fried twelve eggs till the whites were runny and the yolks were hard, and jammed the whole lot into the sandwich.

"Salt?" said the polecat.

Jack took a double handful of salt from the jar and spread a thick layer of it over the sandwich filling.

"Enough?" he said.

"More," said the polecat.

Jack spread on the same again. *"Voilà!"* he said, arranging the sandwich on a huge plate. "Sandwich à la enormous!"

There was now a scratching and a sniffing at the door. A very large scratching. In fact, a *gigantic* scratching.

SCRATCH
SCRATCH

"Staff Entrance, as usual," said the polecat, wearily. "No brains at *all*."

Jack went to the door and looked out of the spyhole ... and took a very quick step back.

"Well?" said Anna. "What is it?"

Jack was white as paper. His mouth opened, but no sound came out.

"One of them, you know, fings," said the polecat, very sly. "Little front legs, big back legs."

"Big long tail?" said Anna, in her Wildlife Expert voice.

"That's the one," said the polecat.

"A kangaroo," said Anna. "How *sweet*!"

"Hey!" said Jack, finding his voice.

Too late. Anna had whipped the plate out of his hands and jerked open the door.

THE KANGAROO
SENDS IT BACK

"It's a very big kangaroo,"
Anna said, in a peculiar voice.

"But it's *green*," said Jack,
in another peculiar voice.

Green it was, and scaly, and
so huge that its head filled up the
whole door.

There was a mouth and a fierce
little eye. The mouth opened,

showing teeth half a metre long and
filling the kitchen with smelly breath.

"Can't get in," said the polecat.
"*Hates* not getting in. Hangs around
outside, bothering me customers."

Anna said, in a shaky voice,
"Here, Kanga," and threw the
sandwich into the mouth, which
closed with a snap.

There was a moment's silence.
Then the mouth said *ptoo*! and the
kitchen was full of bits of spat-out
sandwich. Then the head was gone.

"Didn't seem to like his lunch," said the polecat, strolling out of the burrow. Gingerly, Jack and Anna tiptoed out after him.

There was a good view from the

café, of a slope of ground leading
out of the wood and on to a great
plain. Halfway across the plain,
a huge animal was running away
as fast as it could go.

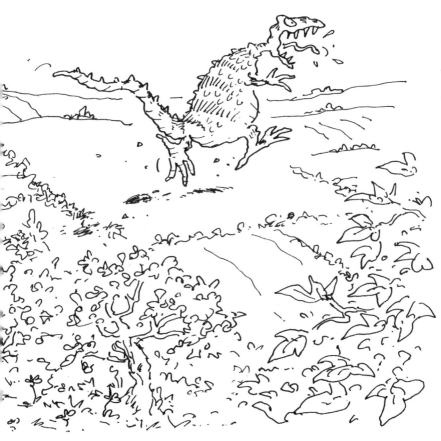

As it ran, it pawed its mouth, as
if trying to get rid of something that
tasted awful.

Jack said, "That's not a kangaroo. That's a Tyrannosaurus Rex!"

"That's it," said the polecat. "Came out of the caves over the way. 'orribly old, terrible manners. Riff-raff, in short. Good riddance to bad rubbish, says I."

"But Tyrannosaurus Rex is the hungriest animal *ever*," said Anna.

"You'd have to be hungry to eat *that* sandwich," said the polecat. "Hungrier than any animal *I've* ever met. Well, can't stand here talking all day. Got me teas to think about."

Can't stand here talking all day.

"You let me make that sandwich on purpose," said Jack.

"You let me open that door on purpose," said Anna.

But the polecat had gone into his café and closed the door, and this time he had locked it behind him.

The sun came out. Somehow neither Jack nor Anna was at all cross any more. But neither of them said anything for some time.

Finally, Jack said, "I'm still going to be a Chef. But I might get some, er, *lessons*."

Anna said, "I'm still going to be a Wildlife Expert... But I might get, er, *a book*."

I might get lessons.

I might get a book.

And they hiked back
home for tea.